This igloo book belongs to:

....

igl00books

Published in 2019
by Igloo Books Ltd,
Cottage Farm,
Sywell,
NN6 0BJ
www.igloobooks.com

Illustrated by Belinda Strong

Designed by Kerri-Ann Hulme
Edited by Helen Catt

1019 003
6 8 10 12 11 9 7 5
ISBN 978-1-78670-295-1

Printed and manufactured in China

My First
Bedtime Rhymes

igloobooks

Twinkle, Twinkle, Little Star

Twinkle, twinkle, little star,
How I wonder what you are.
Up above the world so high,
Like a diamond in the sky.
Twinkle, twinkle, little star,
How I wonder what you are.

The Balloon

What is the news of the day,
Good neighbour, I pray?
They say the balloon,
Is gone up to the moon.
That is the news of the day.

A Star

Higher than a house,
Higher than a tree.
Oh, whatever can that be?
A star.

Starlight, Star Bright

Starlight, star bright,
The first star I see tonight.
I wish I may, I wish I might,
Have the wish I wish tonight.

The Owl and the Pussycat

The owl and the pussycat went to sea,
In a beautiful pea-green boat.
They took some honey and plenty of money,
Wrapped up in a five pound note.

The owl looked up to the stars above,
And sang to a small guitar.
"Oh, lovely pussy. Oh, pussy, my love.
What a beautiful pussy you are, you are.
What a beautiful pussy you are."

Pussy said to the owl, "You elegant fowl,
How charmingly sweet you sing.
Oh, let us be married, too long we have tarried,
But what shall we do for a ring?"

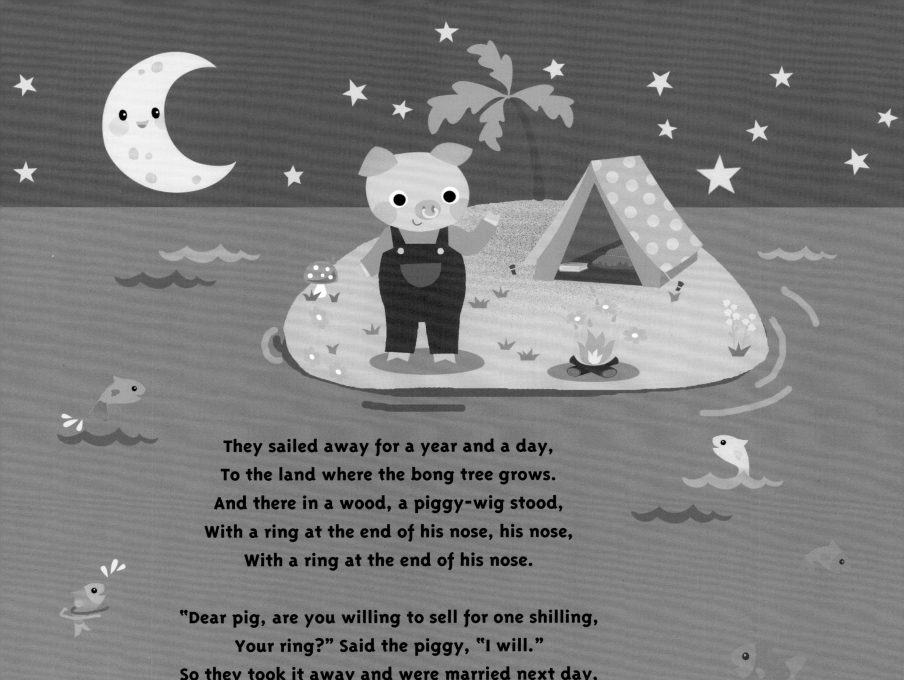

They sailed away for a year and a day,
To the land where the bong tree grows.
And there in a wood, a piggy-wig stood,
With a ring at the end of his nose, his nose,
With a ring at the end of his nose.

"Dear pig, are you willing to sell for one shilling,
Your ring?" Said the piggy, "I will."
So they took it away and were married next day,
By the turkey who lives on the hill.

They dined on mince and slices of quince,
Which they ate with a runcible spoon.
And hand in hand, on the edge of the sand,
They danced by the light of the moon, the moon,
They danced by the light of the moon.

There Was an Old Woman Who Lived in a Shoe

There was an old woman who lived in a shoe.

She had so many children, she didn't know what to do.

She gave them some soup and slices of bread.

She hugged them and kissed them,

Then put them to bed.

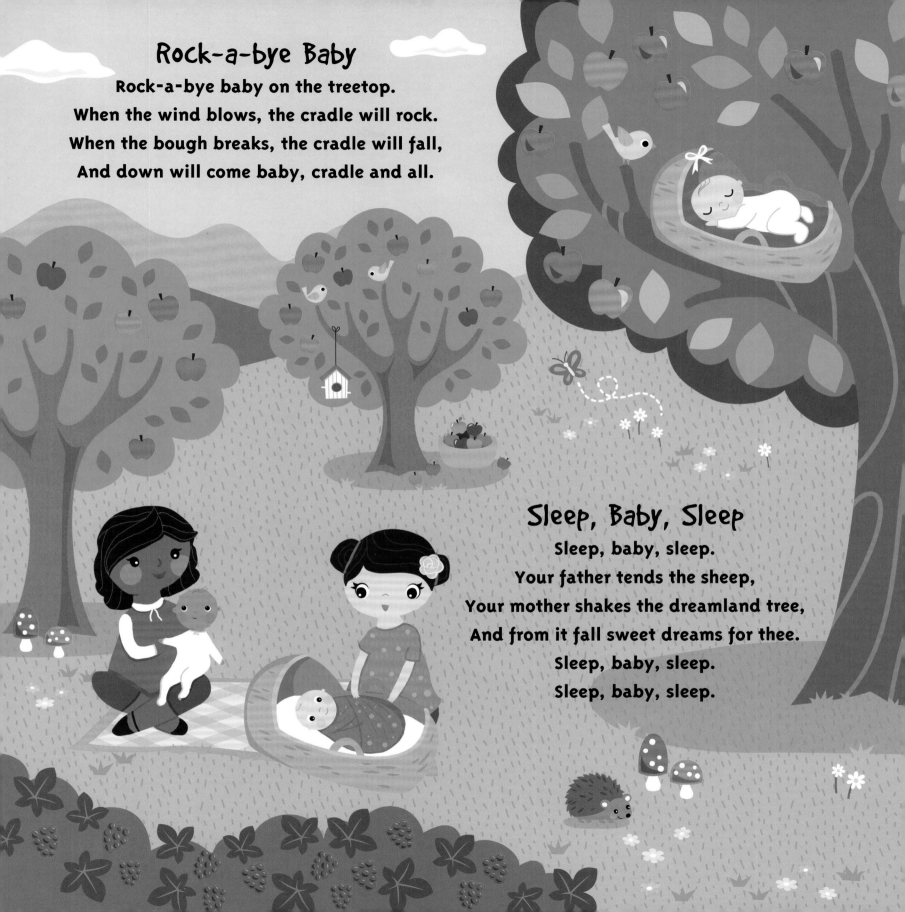

Rock-a-bye Baby

Rock-a-bye baby on the treetop.
When the wind blows, the cradle will rock.
When the bough breaks, the cradle will fall,
And down will come baby, cradle and all.

Sleep, Baby, Sleep

Sleep, baby, sleep.
Your father tends the sheep,
Your mother shakes the dreamland tree,
And from it fall sweet dreams for thee.
Sleep, baby, sleep.
Sleep, baby, sleep.

Babies

Come to the land where the babies grow,
Like flowers in the green, green grass.
Tiny babes that swing and crow,
Whenever the warm winds pass,
And laugh at their own bright eyes aglow,
In a fairy looking glass.

Come to the sea where the babies sail,
In ships of shining pearl.
Borne to the west by a golden gale,
Of sunbeams all awhirl,
And perhaps a baby brother will sail,
To you, my little girl.

Row, Row, Row Your Boat

Row, row, row your boat,
Gently down the stream.
Merrily, merrily,
Merrily, merrily.
Life is but a dream.
Row, row, row your boat,
Gently down the stream.
If you see a crocodile,
Don't forget to scream.

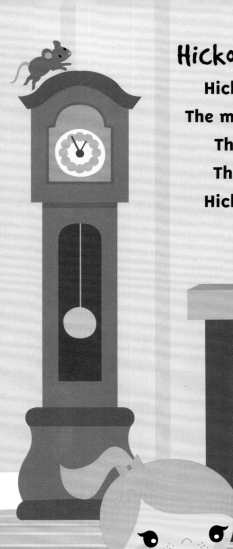

Hickory, Dickory, Dock

Hickory, dickory, dock.
The mouse ran up the clock.
The clock struck one,
The mouse ran down.
Hickory, dickory, dock.

Fairy Bread

Come up here, oh, dusty feet.
Here is fairy bread to eat.
Here in my retiring room,
Children, you may dine,
On the golden smell of broom,
And the shade of pine.
And when you have eaten well,
Fairy stories hear and tell.

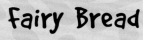

Jack be Nimble

Jack be nimble,
Jack be quick.
Jack jump over
The candlestick.

I See the Moon

I see the moon,
And the moon sees me.
God bless the moon,
And God bless me.

The Man in the Moon

The man in the moon came tumbling down,
And asked the way to Norwich.
He went by the south and burned his mouth,
With eating cold pease porridge.

Norwich

Early to Bed

Early to bed,
Early to rise.
Makes little Johnny,
Wealthy and wise.

Girls and Boys, Come Out to Play

Girls and boys, come out to play.

The moon will shine as bright as day.

Leave your supper and leave your sleep,

And come with your play friends into the street.

Come with a whoop, come with a call.

Come with a good will or not at all.

Up the ladder and down the wall,

A halfpenny roll will serve us all.

You'll find milk and I'll find flour,

And we'll have a pudding in half an hour.

The Moon

The moon is round,
As round can be.
Two eyes, a nose,
And a mouth, like me.

Wee Willie Winkie

Wee Willie Winkie runs through the town,
Upstairs and downstairs in his nightgown.
Tapping at the window, crying through the lock,
"Are all the children in their beds,
Now it's eight o'clock?"

The Animal Fair

I went to the animal fair,
The birds and the beasts were there.
The big baboon by the light of the moon,
Was combing his auburn hair.

You ought to have seen the monkey,
He jumped on the elephant's trunk.
The elephant sneezed and fell to his knees,
And what became of the monkey?

Come to the Window

Come to the window,
My baby, with me,
And look at the stars,
That shine on the sea.

There are two little stars,
That play bo-peep,
With two little fish,
Far down in the deep.

And two little frogs,
Cry, "Neap, neap, neap."
I see a dear baby,
That should be asleep.

Grandmother Grundy

Oh, Grandmother Grundy,
Now what would you say,
If the katydids carried,
Your glasses away?

Carried them off,
To the top of the sky,
And used them to watch,
The eclipses go by?

Sippity Sup

Sippity sup, sippity sup,
Bread and milk from a china cup.
Bread and milk from a bright silver spoon,
Made of a piece of the bright silver moon.
Sippity sup, sippity sup,
Sippity, sippity sup.

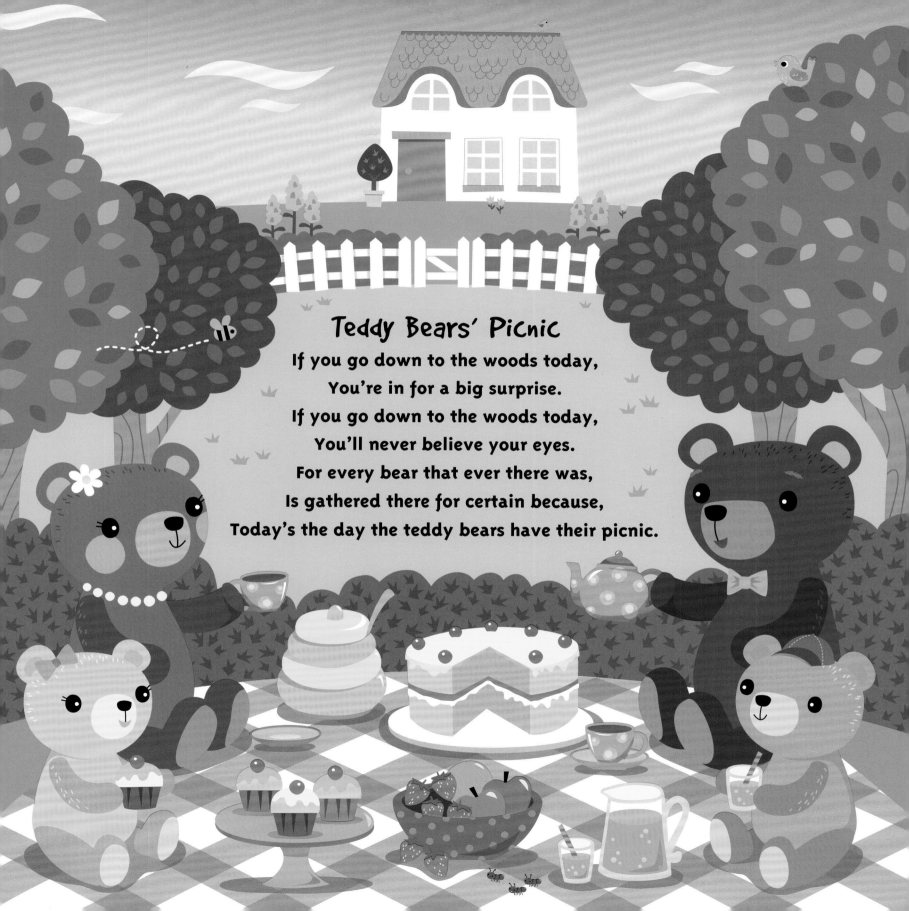

Teddy Bears' Picnic

If you go down to the woods today,
You're in for a big surprise.
If you go down to the woods today,
You'll never believe your eyes.
For every bear that ever there was,
Is gathered there for certain because,
Today's the day the teddy bears have their picnic.

There Were Ten in the Bed

There were ten in the bed and the little one said,
"Roll over. Roll over."
So they all rolled over and one fell out.

There were nine in the bed and the little one said,
"Roll over. Roll over."
So they all rolled over and one fell out.

There were eight in the bed and the little one said,
"Roll over. Roll over."
So they all rolled over and one fell out.

There were seven in the bed and the little one said,
"Roll over. Roll over."
So they all rolled over and one fell out.

There were six in the bed and the little one said,
"Roll over. Roll over."
So they all rolled over and one fell out.

There were five in the bed and the little one said,
"Roll over. Roll over."
So they all rolled over and one fell out.

There were four in the bed and the little one said,
"Roll over. Roll over."
So they all rolled over and one fell out.

There were three in the bed and the little one said,
"Roll over. Roll over."
So they all rolled over and one fell out.

There were two in the bed and the little one said,
"Roll over. Roll over."
So they all rolled over and one fell out.

There was one in the bed and the little one said,
"Goodnight."

Hey, Diddle, Diddle

Hey, diddle, diddle,
The cat and the fiddle.
The cow jumped over the moon.
The little dog laughed to see such fun,
And the dish ran away with the spoon.

Hippity-hop to Bed

Oh, it's hippity-hop to bed.
I'd rather sit up instead,
But when Father says, "Must,"
There's nothing but just,
Go hippity-hop to bed.

Goodnight, Sleep Tight

Goodnight, sleep tight.
Wake up bright,
In the morning light,
To do what's right,
With all your might.